This **Picture Mammoth** *belongs to*

BRUNSWICK PARK PRIMARY
PICTON STREET
CAMBERWELL
LONDON SE5 7QH

For Joseph
A.C.

For my mum
R.A.

ELLA AND THE NAUGHTY LION

written by

ANNE COTTRINGER

pictures by

RUSSELL AYTO

picture Mammoth

The day Ella's mother
    came home with baby Jasper, a lion
    slipped in through the door.

He was a very naughty lion.

He pulled off Jasper's blanket.

He crept into Jasper's cot
and stretched out in a long yawn.
There was no room for Jasper.

When Ella's mother fed Jasper, the lion roared
so loudly, the whole house shook.

The lion tore up Jasper's soft brown teddy

and then chewed it into little wet bits.

"Naughty lion," said Ella. "That was Jasper's favourite teddy! Don't you ever do that again!"

But sometimes the lion was a good lion.
When Ella's grandmother took Ella out
for the day, the lion went too.
He wasn't a naughty lion at all.

He slid down the slide with Ella.

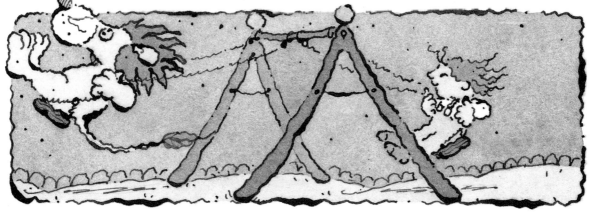

He swung on the swing.

He got dizzy from whizzing round the roundabout with Ella and her friends.

But when they got home, the lion
jumped into Jasper's bath . . .

and splashed water
all over the bathroom.

The next day, Jasper had
the snuffles and couldn't get to sleep.
He was very grizzly.

Ella wanted her mother to
play zoos with her.

"I can't, Ella. I'm too busy
with Jasper," said her mother.

"Why don't you go to the supermarket
with Daddy and maybe he'll buy
something nice to eat!"

But Ella didn't want anything nice to eat.
She was very unhappy. So was the lion,
and he was naughtier than ever!

He galloped up and down the aisles.

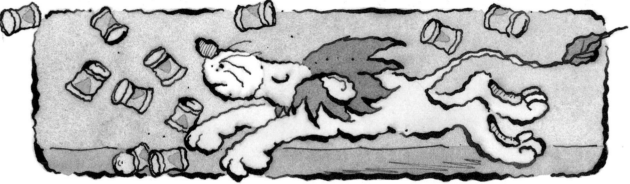

He knocked over stacks of baked beans

and crashed through a pyramid of oranges.

He gobbled up some cakes and got pink icing
all over his whiskers.

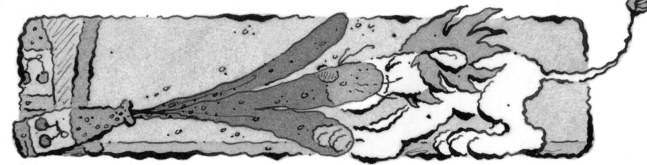

He spilled a big bottle of fizzy red cherryade
that spurted like a fountain over everything.

He roared so loudly that he frightened all
the people at the checkout.

"Bad, bad, bad lion!" Ella scolded him all the way home.
"Don't you ever behave like that again!"

When they got home,
Jasper was asleep in his pram.
Ella's father squeezed past with
his shopping bags.

The naughty lion bounded in behind him and
bumped Jasper's pram.

It started
to roll

towards the
open door,

and before
anyone
knew it,

the pram was
bouncing down
the steps.

Ella and the lion watched with wide eyes.
Then the lion roared a big roar.

In a flash, Ella leaped
and caught hold of Jasper as
he sailed through the air.

Ella's mother and father rushed out.
"Oh Ella! What would we do
without you!" cried her mother.
"Well done," said her father.
The lion growled deep down
inside his throat.

Ella's mother
made some
hot chocolate.

Ella sat on the sofa
with Jasper gurgling
happily in her arms.
Ella smiled at her
baby brother and
gave his rattle
a little shake.

The lion got a
very grumpy look
on his face.
He flicked his
tail back and forth,
but Ella didn't notice.

And so the lion
slipped out just as
he had come in.

But from time to
time Ella heard a little
growl at the door.

First published in Great Britain 1996
by WH Books Ltd
Published 1997 by Mammoth
an imprint of Reed International Books Limited
Michelin House, 81 Fulham Road, London, SW3 6RB
and Auckland, Melbourne, Singapore and Toronto

Text copyright © Anne Cottringer 1996
Illustrations copyright © Russell Ayto 1996
The author and illustrator have asserted their moral rights

ISBN 0 7497 3019 6

A CIP catalogue record for this title
is available from the British Library

Produced by Mandarin Offset Ltd
Printed in Hong Kong

Seven of the Best

Cat's Colours
Jane Cabrera
ISBN 0 7497 3120 6

Do Pigs Have Stripes?
Melanie Walsh
ISBN 0 7497 3026 9

Ella and the Naughty Lion
Russell Ayto and Anne Cottringer
ISBN 0 7497 3019 6

I Like It When
Mary Murphy
ISBN 0 7497 3119 2

When Martha's Away
Bruce Ingman
ISBN 0 7497 2957 0

Mouse Creeps
Reg Cartwright and Peter Harris
ISBN 0 7497 3123 0

Wolf
Sara Fanelli
ISBN 0 7497 2870 1

(*)

picture mammoth